W9-BTO-441

Dear Parents:

Congratulations! Your child is taking the first steps on an exciting journey. The destination? Independent reading!

STEP INTO READING® will help your child get there. The program offers five steps to reading success. Each step includes fun stories and colorful art or photographs. In addition to original fiction and books with favorite characters, there are Step into Reading Non-Fiction Readers, Phonics Readers and Boxed Sets, Sticker Readers, and Comic Readers—a complete literacy program with something to interest every child.

Learning to Read, Step by Step!

Ready to Read   Preschool–Kindergarten
• big type and easy words • rhyme and rhythm • picture clues
For children who know the alphabet and are eager to begin reading.

Reading with Help   Preschool–Grade 1
• basic vocabulary • short sentences • simple stories
For children who recognize familiar words and sound out new words with help.

Reading on Your Own   Grades 1–3
• engaging characters • easy-to-follow plots • popular topics
For children who are ready to read on their own.

Reading Paragraphs   Grades 2–3
• challenging vocabulary • short paragraphs • exciting stories
For newly independent readers who read simple sentences with confidence.

Ready for Chapters   Grades 2–4
• chapters • longer paragraphs • full-color art
For children who want to take the plunge into chapter books but still like colorful pictures.

STEP INTO READING® is designed to give every child a successful reading experience. The grade levels are only guides; children will progress through the steps at their own speed, developing confidence in their reading. The F&P Text Level on the back cover serves as another tool to help you choose the right book for your child.

Remember, a lifetime love of reading starts with a single step!

Step into Reading, Random House, and the Random House colophon are registered trademarks of Penguin Random House LLC.

Visit us on the Web!
StepIntoReading.com
randomhousekids.com

Educators and librarians, for a variety of teaching tools, visit us at
RHTeachersLibrarians.com

Library of Congress Cataloging-in-Publication Data
Berenstain, Stan.
The Berenstain Bears by the sea / The Berenstains.
   p. cm. — (Step into reading. A step 2 book)
Summary: The Bear family goes to the beach, but before they can swim in the ocean there's a lot of work to be done.
ISBN 978-0-679-88719-5 (trade) — ISBN 978-0-679-98719-2 (lib. bdg.) —
ISBN 978-0-553-53698-0 (ebook)
[1. Beaches—Fiction. 2. Bears—Fiction. 3. Stories in rhyme.]
I. Berenstain, Jan. II. Title. III. Series: Step into reading. Step 2 book.
PZ7.B4483 Bemkc 2003 [E]—dc21 2002013674

Printed in the United States of America 32 31 30 29

This book has been officially leveled by using the F&P Text Level Gradient™ Leveling System.

The Berenstain Bears

BY THE SEA

The Berenstains

Random House 🏠 New York

Is it far,
Papa Bear?

Those seagulls mean
we'll soon be there.

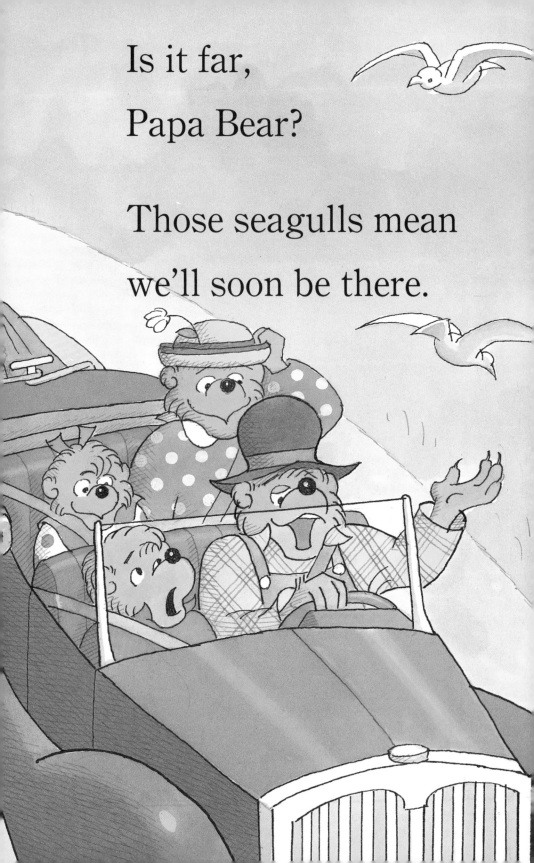

There is the house
where we will stay.
Our shore vacation
starts today!

The wind was strong.
It opened the door.
Sand blew in
upon the floor!
This house was empty
for a while.
Each room has
its own sand pile.

Let's put on suits
and go in the water.

Not yet, son!
Not yet, daughter!

We must clean up,
room by room.
Here's a dustpan.
Here's a broom.

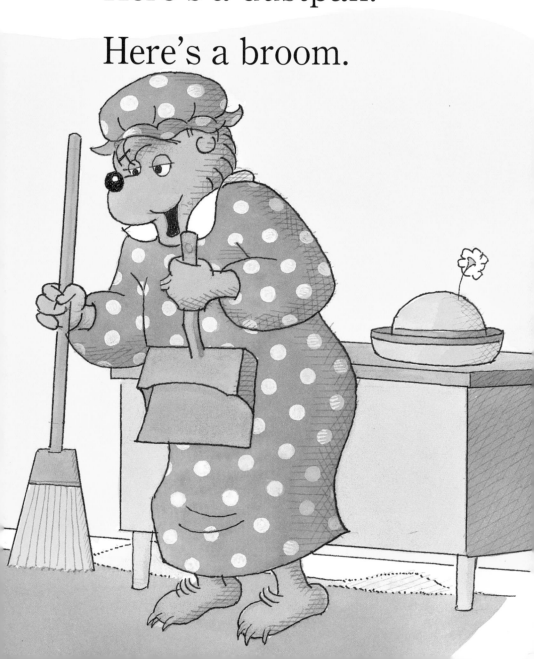

Now the clean-up
job is done.

It's time to have
some ocean fun.

Not just yet!
There's more to be done
before you start
your ocean fun.

There are

things to carry,

beds to make,

closets to clean,

walks to rake.

Mama, all of
that is done.
<u>Now</u> may we start
our ocean fun?

May we? May we?
May we, please,
dip our tootsies
in the seas?

Will you please relax!

You've got all day.

The ocean will

not go away.

There are many things
we must unpack.
Then we'll have
our little snack.

Mama, our little
snack is done.
<u>Now</u> may we start
our ocean fun?

Dears, it's much
too soon after food.

Rats and phooey!

Now, let's not be rude!

It's long after snacks.

May we go in soon?

It's getting late

in the afternoon!

That's why we're here,
to swim in the ocean.
But first, my dears,
let's put on some lotion.

At last we can go
into the water!

Wait, my son!
Wait, my daughter!

But, Papa! Will we never swim in the sea?

Relax! I just wanted you
to wait for me.

Come on, cubs!

Shake a leg!

Last one in
is a rotten egg!

The ocean is fun!
The ocean is great!
It may even have been
worth the wait!